NorMaN
THe CaterpiLLar

By
JoHNNy MacKay

For Johnny

*"Mackay has created a magical
and precious world."*
- Eoin Colfer

"I feel as though Johnny Mackay wrote my autobiography."
- Stephen Fry

*"Norman is my kind of caterpillar.
A truly wonderful story."*
- Sandi Toksvig

www.johnnyshappyplace.com

Once upon a time there lived a caterpillar. His name was Norman. Norman Freeman.

He was a regular looking caterpillar: plump, green and a little spiky, yet there was one thing that was unusual about Norman: he went everywhere backwards.

Kids in the forest would often make fun of him. Sometimes the bats would keep him awake at night singing:

"NOR-MAN THE BORE-MAN, CRAWLING ON THE FLOOR-MAN!"

"IF YOU GO ANY SLOWER YOU'LL BE GOING FORWARDS!"

the crows would caw.

He kinda liked the attention but it got a bit irritating. Folk liked Norman, but in the forest there was one creature above all who adored him.

Cynthia was a snail; a rather beautiful snail. Others saw Norman as weird whereas Cynthia found him fascinating. She liked his style and the way he moved; she found his movement graceful and hypnotic; she loved to behold him.

One day Cynthia was sliding across the forest floor on her way to the stream. Norman was approaching, following the trail Cynthia had made; he was on his way to find some new leaves for breakfast. Cynthia saw Norman coming as his little bum crept up alongside her; she tingled inside and her little heart started to beat incredibly fast; slime rushed to her face and she began to blush.

"Hiya Cynth!" Norman cried.

"Oh, hiya Norm!" replied Cynthia, "didn't see you there!"

Although Norman was one of the slowest creatures in the forest, compared to Cynthia he was a real boy racer. Whenever they met, she always secretly wished that he would stay longer so she could admire him more, but he seemed to always be in a hurry.

"You up to much today Norman?"

"Today is the same as everyday Cynthia," he replied, "I'm turning over a new leaf!"

"Oh Norman, stop it. Turning over a new leaf! I don't know, honestly! What are you like? You really are something else!!"

Norman looked up at the sky, hoping for inspiration to find something interesting to talk to Cynthia about, but nothing came.

"What do you mean I'm something else?" Norman said, nervously passing the conversation back to Cynthia.

"I don't know Norm, I guess you just tickle me that's all. You've got a funny bone. You make people laugh! You do me anyway."

"But I don't have any bones," said Norman.

"See what I mean Norm? You're hilarious, stop it, you'll crack me up!!"

They both laughed.

"I guess I'd better get going then," Norman said abruptly. "It's been nice seeing you Cynthia, I'll see you around."

"Oh. Ok. Bye then Norm."

Before he could get away Cynthia called him.

"Norman!"

"Yes Cynthia?" inching his way back, having already covered the length of a fully-grown worm in a matter of seconds.

"Yes?"

Their bodies were now only a baby woodlouse in length apart.

"Norman, why are you in a rush all the time? Are you in a hurry?"

"Er... No...?"

"So why shoot off so quick? Do you not like my company?"

Norman felt a pain in his tummy. He didn't feel good that Cynthia thought he didn't like her.

"Cynthia no...of course not for heavens sake, why do you think that?"

"Well, it's only ever so brief when we bump into each other, you and I, Norman. I like you. You're different."

"Really?" said Norman.

"Yeah!"

Norman felt good, but a little sad. He didn't know Cynthia liked him so much. Norman liked Cynthia too.

"You see Norman, I rarely get time to see anyone these days, and I'm not too keen on many other snails. They're nice enough but they're a bit slow, if you know what I mean. Most creatures whizz by me before I know it and then all I see is the back of their heads! You Norm, I get to look at your face even after we've said goodbye, so even though I love to say hello, saying goodbye is nice too, because I can still see you, and I love your face!"

"You do?" replied Norman.

"I really do. You're beautiful."

Norman started to blush. Cynthia had never seen him blush before. She instinctively seized the moment to ask him a question she'd wanted to for ages.

"Why do you go backwards?"

Norman was a little taken aback with her forthrightness.

"I don't know?"

"You must!" said Cynthia.

"I don't!" replied Norman.

"Don't you want to know what is ahead of you?"

"Of course."

"So why?"

"I don't know!"

"You must do!" exclaimed Cynthia. "Do you not bump into things?"

"Yep."

"Does it hurt?"

"Yeah."

"Oh Norman."

Cynthia looked deeply into his eyes, trying to see what it was that he was hiding. She smiled and that made Norman smile. They stood in the undergrowth simply smiling, and just for a short time, words didn't matter.

"You know Norm, you don't have to rush anywhere. There isn't anything to be worried about."

"OK," said Norman, "thank you, I'll bear that in mind."

Norman bowed to Cynthia in a parting gesture.

"Thanks again Cynthia."

He had reached the brow of a molehill when Cynthia shouted.

"NORMAN!"

"YES CYNTHIA?"

"DONT FORGET!"

"WHAT'S THAT?!"

"YOU'RE SPECIAL!"

Norman's heart skipped a beat and he felt a surge of energy run through his body. In that moment he felt like he could do anything at all. He felt alive!

Then, suddenly, the earth began to rumble and shake. Norman lost his footing and began to tumble down the molehill. Slightly embarrassed, and covered in dirt, he got back on his feet when promptly a mole popped his head out.

"Whoever it was that was on my mound, I kindly ask that you refrain from using my home as a look out point or whatever you were up here for. I find it hard enough as it is being blind let alone fending off intruders. Surely you can find a place of your

...and back down he went.

Norman quickly got going, hoping that no one had seen him fall! He headed in any direction, adrenaline pumping through his little body, but as he began to calm down he noticed something odd.

He was facing the way he was going.

He was going forward!

For the first time in his life he was moving forward like normal caterpillars were supposed to. Pride welled up inside, but that was soon replaced.

Fear.

He wanted to turn back; carry on as before.

Frozen, with those choices, Norman faced the inevitable. He channelled all the energy he could muster and with gritted teeth charged forward, not knowing what he would encounter. Whatever it was that lay ahead he knew that he could not give up and he certainly could not go back.

Later that day Norman tucked himself under a moss covered twig to rest, but the longer he lay there the angrier he became. He was annoyed for not believing in himself enough.

As it turned out, Norman was able to climb the giant boulder he never dared climb before. The tree stump and the gatepost were fairly easy to overcome too, as was everything else he encountered.

"Why have I doubted myself and why am I always rushing? What am I searching for? Eating leaves day after day? Really? Is that all there is?! Where can I find what I'm looking for??"

Unable to find an answer to his questions he became even more furious. Feeling suffocated under the twig, he drew back the moss, stepped outside and took a deep breath of fresh air.

"Yes I am tiny, I get that, but why do I have to feel so small?"

Norman began to climb a tree, heading for the top.

"The birds know how to fly and the spider knows how to spin its web. What am I meant to do?"

Norman found a nice branch.

"I'm not having it! I'm not being small anymore!"

He was determined not to come down until he had worked things out.

That night Cynthia tucked herself up tight in her shell. She had a funny, fuzzy feeling in her tummy. The next day she planned to go and find Norman, tell him that she loved him and ask him if he would like to spend a lot more time together.

In the morning, Cynthia set off to find him. She looked for Norman everywhere but he was nowhere to be seen. After a few hours Cynthia began to ask around.

"Excuse me, Mr Robin, have you seen Norman?"

"That caterpillar that crawls backwards? My dear if he doesn't know where he is going how do I know where he has been? I wouldn't touch him with a barge pole and no I ain't seen him love, sorry."

...Cynthia carried on searching.

"LEFT, LEFT, LEFT RIGHT LEFT! LEFT, LEFT, LEFT RIGHT LEFT!!"

Cynthia encountered an army of ants.

"Excuse me?"

They were too loud marching to hear her.

"EXCUSE ME!" Cynthia shouted.

The ants stood to attention.

"YES MA'AM!!" shouted the Commander.

"I'm sorry to bother you, but I am looking for a friend and I cannot find him."

"ARE YOU NOTIFYING MY BRIGADE OF A MISSING PERSON MA'AM?" the Commander enquired.

"Er, yes I think so," replied Cynthia.

"OK, ANY REMARKABLE FEATURES ABOUT THIS PERSON? HOW MANY EYES DOES HE HAVE? CLAWS, PAWS, BEAK ETC?"

"Well his name is Norman and he is a caterpillar."

"NORMAN THE CATERPILLAR MA'AM?" he reiterated.

"Yes."

"YES I KNOW OF THE CREATURE. WITH RESPECT MA'AM, IF A GROWN CATERPILLAR MARCHES EVERYWHERE BACKWARDS, DO YOU NOT THINK IT IS INEVITABLE THAT HE WILL GET LOST?"

Cynthia was lost for words.

"OUR PATHS HAVE CROSSED BEFORE," said the ant. "I HAVE TOLD NORMAN TO HIS FACE, 'YOU NEED DISCIPLINE BOY. IT'S NO LIFE FUMBLING ALONG LIKE THIS. JOIN US. WORK FOR YOUR QUEEN AND COUNTRY. HAVE PURPOSE', BUT OF COURSE HE DECLINED OUR OFFER. HE DOESN'T WANT PURPOSE IN HIS LIFE, MA'AM. WE HAVE MORE IMPORTANT THINGS TO DO THAN LOOK AFTER YOUR FRIEND."

Cynthia's heart sank.

"HOWEVER, IF WE DO COME ACROSS HIM, YOU HAVE MY WORD THAT WE WILL CARRY HIM BACK TO YOU. NOW LET ME TAKE SOME CONTACT DETAILS."

Cynthia was thankful for their cooperation.

After a bit more searching, Cynthia came across the pigeons sitting side by side on a branch.

"Hello," Cynthia said warmly.

"Oo helloo, what can we dooo for yooo?" *cooed* one of the pigeons.

"I was just wondering if any of you had seen Norman? I have been searching for him all day and I can't find *him* anywhere...

...I've asked everyone but there is no trace of him. Please?"

"Why is a snail looking for a caterpillar anyway?" the pigeon asked.

"Look, I am simply asking if you have seen him. Have you or not??"

After a long and uncomfortable silence the oldest pigeon coughed up.

"I have seen him."

"Where??" asked Cynthia.

"Climbing up a tree?"

"Which tree?" asked Cynthia.

"I cannot recall?"

"Where abouts was this tree?"

"I do not recall?"

"You must!"

"My dear, I am old and you are fortunate I can remember anything at all."

"I need to find him," said Cynthia desperately.

The old pigeon fidgeted.

"Well I need peace and quiet. Toddle on now and please have respect for your elders. Manners cost nothing you know?"

Cynthia headed off when almost out of earshot the pigeon chirped up, like it had just startled itself out of a deep sleep.

"Oh yes and one more thing my dear."

Cynthia turned her head back.

"He was moving."

"Moving?" replied Cynthia.

"Yes, moving, head first, in a proper fashion. Then again it might have been a dream; I am old and cannot tell what is real and what is imaginary anymore."

Cynthia paused, not knowing what to make of what she had just been told, yet after a few moments she carried on her way. Even though Cynthia wasn't sure of where she was going she was determined not to stop until she had found Norman. But as day crept into night, Cynthia slid around in a puddle of her own tears, up and down and round and round the forest, searching.

As morning came and the sun rose, Cynthia stared at the crimson circle in the sky and made a wish.

"Please send me an angel
to lift me up."

Cynthia had run out of tears; she didn't know you
could run out of tears. She felt empty and her
head slumped in exhaustion. As she fell asleep a
gentle breeze and calmness surrounded her. She

started to dream. In Cynthia's dream Norman was searching for her, just as she had been searching for him. Even though she was sleeping she was aware that she was asleep. She had never experienced a lucid dream before; it was as though it wasn't a dream at all. A stronger breeze began to stir her from her slumber. She could hear Norman calling her name. It sounded so real.

"Cynth, it's Norman!"

Cynthia was awake now but was too afraid to open her eyes. She felt serene. The breeze on her face encouraged her lids to open.

"Norman," Cynthia whispered.

"Cynthia!" Norman exclaimed.

"Norm! Where have you been?"

"Cynthia! Look! Look at me!"

Cynthia blinked, trying to focus her sleepy eyes.

"I'm a bird Cynthia, look!"

"My word! You're... you're... a butterfly!"

"I am??"

"You are," she said, "you're a butterfly Norman, but that's..." Cynthia couldn't finish her words. She was flabbergasted.

Norman began to slowly raise the pair of wings; a kaleidoscope of colours pointing upwards, almost touching each other. They were huge, with intricate patterns swirling all around them!

"Where did you get them??" asked Cynthia.

"I didn't get them!" replied Norman. "I had them all along! I guess I just needed time to find them! Aren't they wonderful!?"

"Yes, they are Norman!" replied Cynthia. "Truly wonderful!! I can't believe it. You're here." Cynthia sobbed, finding a new reserve of tears only used for the happiest of times.

"I'm here alright," Norman beamed proudly. His newfound confidence overflowing!

"What on earth shall we do now?" Cynthia wondered.

Norman moved closer.

"Cynthia, I want to be with you forever and fly around the universe! You up for it??"

"Of course I am!" she exclaimed. "YES! Yes, I'm with you Norman!"

Cynthia looked up. There, floating high up in the sky was a red balloon.

Cynthia pointed with her antennae.

"Look Norman!"

"Wow!" said Norman. "A balloon!"

"I want to pop it!" said Cynthia.

"OK then, let's go!"

Norman had no objections! He carefully held onto Cynthia's shell and up they went, over the trees they soared, higher and higher. They saw where they lived and all the beauty that surrounded them.

"Whoopee!!!"

The balloon was getting bigger and bigger. As they got close Norman hoiked Cynthia up so she could position herself, ready to slice the balloon with the underneath of her sharp shell.

"Ready Norman?" asked Cynthia, excitedly.

Norman held his breath and squeezed his eyes tight shut! The friction from the shell and rubber made a terrifying squeal.

BANG!!!

Blasted by the pressure from the explosion, they tumbled, frantically fluttering to regain balance.

Eventually, the intense high-pitched ringing in their ears stopped, and they opened their eyes to see red rubber confetti sprinkling silently all around them. But as Cynthia and Norman delighted in their private ceremony, they were being watched.

A sharp-eyed kestrel peered from high up in the forest canopy, up towards the limitless blue ocean of light in which the newly weds now danced.

However, the kestrel was not eyeing up his prey; he was sharing in their happiness. He knew from experience that it was not impossible to do things that others *thought* impossible.

The kestrel, a member of an exclusive club along with the kingfisher, the hummingbirds and an elite few, could defy the power of the wind, being able to remain as still as the moon at night, high up in the blustery sky, hovering motionlessly with only its beating wings as opposition to the full force of the Gods.

The kestrel knew looks could be deceiving and that what others think of you doesn't have to make you what you are.

What you are comes from the inside.

The kestrel decided not to tell the other animals what he could see. They would just have to wait to see it with their own eyes.

Just like the air inside the balloon,
Cynthia and Norman
were at one with the wind.

The End.

Johnny Mackay was an incredibly passionate human being with a great love of art and creative writing. He was funny, compassionate and a very talented chin balancer - hence the logo! Johnny wrote *Norman the Caterpillar* not long before he died in October 2014 at the age of 29. We knew we had to publish it for him. All of the profits from this book will go towards Johnny's Happy Place which was set up in Johnny's hometown of Kettering, Northamptonshire. It was set up with the desire to help the vulnerable, those with poor mental health and people feeling a bit lost in life. As this book goes to print for the first time, in August 2015, JHP is very much in it's infancy, but we will keep developing and growing. Please visit our website for more details.

www.johnnyshappyplace.com

Passions need to be tempered to purify them;
bring about their beautiful essence.
Passions, if suppressed, bring about nothing good.
They dull the spirit.
Passion is vital for life.
Knowledge and wisdom are lifeless and grey,
like fine food with no flavour.
One needs passion to embrace all life.
Don't be afraid to unleash your inner flame.
Passion is the spark
Love is the wood
Joy is the flame
Peace and happiness is the warmth.

- Johnny Mackay

CPSIA information can be obtained
at www.ICGtesting.com
Printed in the USA
LVOW05s0913011115

460615LV00016B/32/P